The Tricky Rabbit

African-American Trickster Tales

Retold by Walt Flood

SCHOLASTIC INC.
New York Toronto London Auckland Sydney
Mexico City New Delhi Hong Kong Buenos Aires

Illustrations
Nathan Jurevicius

Printed in the U.S.A.

ISBN 0-439-68900-7

7 8 9 10 23 12 11 10 09

Contents

Tiger and Lion have moved in. And they're wrecking Brer Rabbit's fun.

Trouble in the Forest

Brer Rabbit was a young rabbit who lived in the forest. He had a great life. Every day, he'd think of a new joke to play on the other young animals.

Then one day, everything changed. Tiger and Lion moved into the forest, and started eating everything in sight. All the animals hid inside all day, terrified. They

Brer Rabbit loved to play jokes on the other young animals.

didn't dare walk around the forest. And they didn't dare allow their children to play outside.

Brer Rabbit got really bored. He couldn't run outside and shout or laugh. He couldn't hide behind trees and jump out and scare his friends. He just sat at home all day and stared at the wall.

Finally, after days and days of **boredom**, Brer Rabbit couldn't take it anymore. So he came up with a plan.

What do you know so far about Brer Rabbit?

boredom when nothing is interesting or exciting

Brer Rabbit and Tiger meet.
Which one will run away scared?

A Chat With Tiger

The next day, Brer Rabbit went out and found Tiger. Tiger was in the middle of hunting for food, and he looked really hungry.

"Hey, Tiger!" Brer Rabbit called out. "Do you want to fight?"

"What?" Tiger growled.

"I just asked if you're looking for a

"Tiger, I'll make a tiger-skin rug out of you!" Brer Rabbit said.

beating. If you are, I'd be happy to give you one!" Brer Rabbit said.

Tiger couldn't believe his ears. "Rabbit, you're crazy to mess with me!" Tiger said. "I'll eat you in one bite!"

"Oh, really?" Brer Rabbit said. "Just try it! I'll make a tiger-skin rug out of you!"

Tiger was confused. Usually, everyone ran away from him. But this rabbit didn't seem scared at all.

Then Tiger remembered another time that someone hadn't been scared of him. A month before, Tiger had seen a hunter in the forest. The hunter wasn't scared. Why? Because he had a **weapon**!

Maybe this rabbit had a weapon!

Tiger pretended to be calm. "You're all skin and bones," he told Brer Rabbit. "Who would want to eat you anyway?" Then Tiger started to back away.

"Okay, I'll see you later, you **cowardly** Tiger," said Brer Rabbit. "Then I'll get my tiger-skin rug!"

weapon something that can be used in a fight or an attack, such as a gun or a knife

cowardly easily scared

So far, Brer Rabbit's plan is working. But to finish the job, he needs a little help.

Brer Rabbit's Plan

Next, Brer Rabbit went to see Brer Elephant. "Do you want to help me get rid of that tiger?" Brer Rabbit asked.

"I'm not going anywhere near that tiger!" Brer Elephant said. "He'll butter his toast with my brains! He'll use my bones as toothpicks!"

"Oh, calm down, Brer Elephant," Brer

Rabbit said, "and listen to my plan."

"Here's what we'll do," Brer Rabbit said. "I'll ride on your back, and we'll walk past Brer Tiger. When I tap your neck, you'll scream and **trumpet** like crazy. And then, when I pull your ears, you'll scream and fall over like you're dead. Okay?"

"I have just one question," Brer Elephant said. "*Why?*"

"You'll see," said Brer Rabbit.

Why do you think Brer Rabbit wants Brer Elephant's help?

trumpet to make a loud sound

Brer Rabbit and Brer Elephant give Tiger the scare of his life.

Skinning an Elephant

Meanwhile, Tiger was asking around about Brer Rabbit. He soon found out that Brer Rabbit was famous for his tricks and lies. Tiger also found out that the little rabbit didn't have any weapons.

Tiger realized that Brer Rabbit had been **bluffing**. He **vowed** that he'd teach that rabbit a lesson he'd never forget.

bluffing pretending; faking

vowed promised

Not long after, Tiger saw Brer Rabbit riding by on Brer Elephant's back. Tiger tried to be sneaky. "Rabbit," he said, pretending to be nice, "I have something to tell you. Come down from there."

"Hold on, Tiger," Brer Rabbit said. "I'm busy **skinning** this elephant. I'll be finished in a minute."

Tiger wasn't going to let Brer Rabbit fool him again. "Rabbit, do you really think I'm stupid enough to believe that you can skin an elephant?" he asked.

Brer Rabbit didn't answer. Instead, he tapped Brer Elephant on his back. The elephant screamed so loudly that a hundred trees fell over and every bird in the forest laid an egg!

---

skinning taking the skin off of something, usually with a knife

Tiger thought Brer Rabbit might really be skinning that elephant!

Tiger was shocked. He had never heard an elephant scream like that. He stretched his neck to see what Rabbit was doing, but he wasn't tall enough to see.

"Skinning beasts is easy," Brer Rabbit said happily. He tapped the elephant's back again. This time, the elephant's loud trumpeting knocked down two hundred trees and caused every mole in the area to jump out of its hole!

Tiger kept reminding himself that Brer Rabbit was a **trickster**. Still, it really did seem as though the little rabbit was skinning that elephant!

Tiger started to bite his claws nervously. He couldn't help but wonder how it would feel to be skinned alive.

trickster someone who plays a lot of tricks on others

"Brer Rabbit," Tiger said. "**Admit** it. You're not *really* skinning that elephant."

"Just wait until I'm done," Brer Rabbit said merrily. "I'll start skinning you, and *then* you'll believe it."

Tiger tried to act as though he wasn't afraid. But at the same time, he started slowly backing away. "Brer Rabbit, don't be silly. You could never skin me," he said.

"You'd be easy to skin compared to this big elephant," Brer Rabbit answered. "It will be a nice break, actually. And your fur will make such a lovely rug for my friends and me to stomp on."

At that, Brer Rabbit pulled Brer Elephant's ears. Brer Elephant stomped and screamed so loudly that every

admit to confess something

animal in the forest covered its ears, and all the fish in the pond dropped dead from fright!

Then, with a loud thud, Brer Elephant **toppled** over right next to Tiger! Tiger had to jump out of the way to avoid being crushed.

Brer Rabbit landed **gracefully** on the ground and clapped his front paws. "Okay, Tiger," he said. "Are you ready?"

But Tiger had already run right out of the forest.

Do you think Tiger is gone for good? Why or why not?

toppled fell

gracefully smoothly; not clumsily

Tiger has left the forest.
But now Lion is acting up.

King of the Forest

When Lion heard that Tiger had been scared out of the forest, he decided it was time to remind everyone who was boss.

He called all the animals together and said, "I've decided to eat one young animal every day for breakfast." Smacking his lips, he said, "I will pick the juiciest, tastiest young animal from each family."

"I will eat one juicy, tasty child from each family!" Lion said.

All the mothers and fathers began to weep. All the young animals ran to the pond. They looked at their **reflections** to see how juicy and tasty they looked.

But Brer Rabbit only laughed. "Don't worry," he said. "I'll get rid of that lion."

reflections images of things that appear on water and shiny surfaces

Brer Rabbit goes to see Lion. Will the trickster fool Lion, too?

A Chat With Lion

Brer Rabbit knocked on Lion's door. Lion was astonished to see him there. "May I help you?" he asked.

Brer Rabbit pretended to be scared. He said, "Lion, I'm here to ask you a favor. Please gobble me up."

Lion was really **puzzled**. "No one's ever asked me to do that before," he said.

puzzled confused

"You haven't seen the pond beast?" Brer Rabbit asked Lion.

Brer Rabbit explained, "If someone is going to have me for dinner, I'd rather it be you than that beast in the pond."

"What beast in the pond?" Lion asked.

Brer Rabbit faked a look of surprise. "You haven't seen the pond beast? It's twice your size, with teeth twice as big as yours and claws twice as sharp. And when it opens its mouth, its breath smells like lion. I hear it has lion for breakfast, lunch, and dinner."

Now Lion looked **alarmed**. "It eats lions? You must be mistaken, Rabbit! I am the **fiercest** beast in the forest."

"I really wish that were true," Brer Rabbit said sadly.

Lion grabbed Brer Rabbit by the paw. "Take me to the pond and I'll prove it."

"No!" Brer Rabbit shouted. "The Beast will murder you and drink your blood!"

"I'm not scared," Lion said nervously.

alarmed scared

fiercest most violent or dangerous

There's a fight at the pond.
Will Lion win?

Lion Faces a Beast

When Lion and Brer Rabbit reached the pond, Brer Rabbit started jumping and screaming. "Look, Lion!" he yelled. "It's the Pond Beast!"

Lion looked around. "Where is it?" he roared.

Brer Rabbit pointed and yelled, "It's right there. Look in the pond!"

Lion looked into the pond and saw his own reflection.

Lion leaned over and looked into the water. He saw a fierce-looking face with big teeth. Lion jumped back from the pond in fright.

Brer Rabbit started to giggle. The plan was working. Lion didn't realize that he was looking at his own reflection!

Lion roared fiercely at the creature in the water. At the same time, of course, the Pond Beast roared, too.

Lion was scared. But he didn't want Brer Rabbit to tell the other animals that he was a coward. So Lion began insulting the pond beast. "Hey, Pond Beast," Lion roared. "You're the ugliest creature I've ever seen!"

Brer Rabbit was laughing himself silly.

Lion went on, "Pond Beast, you think you're tough, but you're really a wimp. You pretend to be king of the forest, but anyone can see you're just a bully. You're the biggest coward in the forest!"

Brer Rabbit was now rolling on the grass, laughing so hard his stomach hurt.

Lion roared, "Pond Beast, I'll show you who's king of the forest!"

Brer Rabbit watched Lion **swipe** at the water with his paws. Of course, the Pond Beast swiped, too. The more Lion swiped, the more the Pond Beast swiped.

Lion got so mad that he jumped into the pond, clawing all around him! When Lion felt his claws scratching the beast's fur, he almost smiled. But right when he hit the beast, he felt sharp claws stabbing his own flesh! In his **frenzy,** Lion didn't realize he was only scratching himself!

As Lion fought himself, he got more and more hurt and tired. Soon, he was too tired to swim. He sank to the bottom of the pond and drowned.

swipe to hit something or somebody with a hard, sweeping blow

frenzy a state of great excitement

Soon, Lion sank to the bottom of the pond and drowned.

Brer Rabbit ran to tell the other animals the news. They could hardly believe their ears.

"How did you do it, Brer Rabbit?" Brer Bear asked. "How did a little rabbit like you get rid of both Lion and Tiger?"

"I may be a little rabbit," Brer Rabbit said. "But I've got a big brain."

Then off he hopped to think of his next trick.

Do you know anyone like Brer Rabbit?

Glossary

admit *(verb)* to confess something

alarmed *(adjective)* scared

bluffing *(verb)* pretending; faking

boredom *(noun)* when nothing is interesting or exciting

cowardly *(adjective)* easily scared

fiercest *(adjective)* most violent or dangerous *(related words: fierce, fiercely)*

frenzy *(noun)* a state of great excitement

gracefully *(adverb)* smoothly; not clumsily

puzzled *(adjective)* confused

reflections *(noun)* images of things that appear on water and shiny surfaces

skinning *(verb)* taking the skin off of something, usually with a knife

swipe *(verb)* to hit something or somebody with a hard, sweeping blow

toppled *(verb)* fell

trickster *(noun)* someone who plays a lot of tricks on others

trumpet *(verb)* to make a loud sound

vowed *(verb)* promised

weapon *(noun)* something that can be used in a fight or an attack, such as a gun or a knife